This book belongs to:

_____

_____

Contents

First published 2006 by Brown Watson
The Old Mill, 76 Fleckney Road,
Kibworth Beauchamp, Leic LE8 0HG

ISBN: 978-0-7097-1741-6

EARLY READERS

Three Playtime Stories

Stories by Gill Davies

Illustrations by:
Gill Guile, Stephen Holmes,
Jane Swift and Lawrie Taylor

Brown Watson
ENGLAND

SLIDE AND RIDE

Today Rag Doll is very busy. She is giving all the toys a good wash. She sings:

"One two three . . .
This is fun for me.
You'll soon be as clean
As clean can be."

Only Robot is sad. He wants to play too but Rag Doll has forgotten to put him into the water.

Suddenly the soap slips. It slips right out of the water.

"Look out!" shouts Rag Doll. "Look out!" shouts the red boat. "Look out!" shout the yellow duck and the green whale.

As Robot jumps up to see what is going on, the soap slips right under him.

"Yeeeow!" shouts Robot as he goes sliding across the bathroom floor.

9

Then he laughs. Robot laughs
and smiles and then he
sings too.

"One two three . . .
This is fun for me.
I can slide and ride,
Come and play with me."

Soon all the toys get out of
the water and take it in turns
to slide.

"And so now you have
made the floor clean,
too!" laughs Rag Doll.

KEY WORDS

fun	today
him	toys
of	two
out	under
red	wants
right	water
sings	with
three	yellow

WHAT CAN YOU SEE HERE?

robot

bubbles

whale

arm

sink

MRS BOSSY BEAR

Mrs Bossy Bear always tells everyone what to do:

"Don't run on the road . . . Don't wake my baby . . . Don't hold your bat like that, Teddy. . . Don't hit the ball like that, Teddy."

"She is such a bossy Mrs Bossy Bear," says Teddy, as he runs home.

"I must have the best house in town," says Mrs Bossy.
  She paints the house. She even paints the pots red.

  Baby bear sits on the mat. He plays as Mrs Bossy paints.

  The paint drips. The paint drips down. The paint drips down on to baby bear but Mrs Bossy does not see it dripping.

"Oh no!" she says, as she picks up her baby. "Baby has red spots. He must be ill!"

The other bears come to look.

Teddy smiles. "It is paint," he says. "It is just red paint."

Now all the bears smile – even Mrs Bossy. She is so happy she hugs her red spotted baby – and Teddy too.

19

KEY WORDS

ball	red
has	run
in	says
is	see
it	sit
look	the
on	too
play	up

WHAT CAN YOU SEE HERE?

baby

face

paint

pots

window

PICNIC PARTY

Today the animals on the farm are off for a picnic. The sun is shining. The sky is blue. The grass is soft and green. Birds sing in the trees as they trot along.

Then . . ."Oh no!" says Little Red Hen. "It is starting to rain."

"Oh no!" says Woof the dog. "My bones will get wet."

They put the picnic under a big tree to keep dry.

23

"Hello!" say the ducks.
"This rain is fun. Do come
and play with us."

One by one the animals step
out from the trees and begin to
play. Soon they are all having a
good time.

"We like this rain," say the
pigs who love to roll in the
mud. The two dogs jump in
the pond.

Then, as they all play, paddle and splash, at last the sun comes out again.

"Look!" says Grandma Goat. "A rainbow."

Soon the grass is dry again so they all sit down to eat the best picnic they have ever had.

"Thank you," they say to the ducks. "That was fun!" and they give their new friends some bread.

KEY WORDS

are	my
best	new
big	one
come	play
do	rain
good	thank you
grass	tree
little	wet

WHAT CAN YOU SEE HERE?

apples

biscuits

rainbow

cloud

puddles